LITTLE MISS SUNSHINE
on a Rainy Day

Roger Hargreaves

Original concept by
Roger Hargreaves

Written and illustrated by
Adam Hargreaves

Little Miss Sunshine was the sort of person who could see the good side of everything and everyone.

She was the first person to admit that Mr Noisy was very loud.

But wouldn't that be good if you needed someone to shout for help in an emergency?

Mr Fussy might not let you walk across his lawn.

But all that fussiness meant that you could always find what you needed at his house.

Mr Chatterbox might go on and on and on and on and on and on and on and on and on and on and on and on …

… and on!

But wasn't that better than an awkward silence?

Buzzing bees might be a nuisance at a picnic, but without them there would be no yummy honey on toast.

Learning to read might be hard, but how else would you be able to enjoy a good story?

Mowing the grass might seem boring, but how would you play football otherwise?

Now, Mr Grumble was the complete opposite of Little Miss Sunshine, he couldn't see the good in anyone or anything.

And he liked to let everyone know.

Grumble.

Grumble.

Grumble.

He grumbled from morning to night.

Mr Grumble didn't like the morning because he had to get up.

And he didn't like the night because he had to go to bed!

He grumbled
when it was cold.

He grumbled
when it was windy.

He grumbled
when it was foggy.

He grumbled
when it was sunny.

Little Miss Sunshine tried to show him that it was fun to go sledging when it was cold.

It was fun to fly a kite when it was windy.

It was fun to play
hide and seek when
it was foggy.

And it was fun to
go to the beach
when it was hot.

But Mr Grumble
was not convinced.

And Mr Grumble grumbled the very most when it was rainy.

He hated drizzle.

He loathed showers.

He detested downpours.

"But rain is wonderful!" cried Little Miss Sunshine. "You will have to come outside and I will show you."

"I refuse to believe there is anything good about rain!" declared Mr Grumble.

But after much grumbling, Little Miss Sunshine persuaded Mr Grumble to go outdoors.

"First of all, if there was no rain, there wouldn't be any puddles to jump in!" cried Little Miss Sunshine.

SPLASH!

"If there was no rain, there wouldn't be any water to fill the rivers and there wouldn't be any swimming or boating or rope swinging."

"If there was no rain, Mr Perfect's green lawn would be a perfectly brown lawn."

"And Mr Impossible wouldn't be able to grow his record-breaking strawberries."

"Little Miss Naughty needs rain to fill her water balloons and Mr Mischief needs rain to fill his water pistol."

"We need rain running in the gutters to race our paper boats."

And the more Little Miss Sunshine explained to Mr Grumble, the more kindly he began to feel towards rain.

But he wasn't quite there.

"Now, the absolutely best and most wonderful thing about rain," said Little Miss Sunshine.

"Is a rainbow!"

"Now, that is beautiful,"
admitted Mr Grumble.

"Hooray!" cried
Little Miss Sunshine.

"But," said Mr Grumble.

"… it's a bit bright."

"Well then, you'll just have to look on the bright side of life!" laughed Little Miss Sunshine.